For: Madeli[ne]

May you learn many things about Jesus from your mommy and daddy! They are very special friends of mine, and I know you will grow to love them as much as I do! Glad you were born healty, and I can't wait to see you grow up!

Love,
Cherith :)

1-15-05

Annika's Secret Wish

✛

Beverly Lewis

ILLUSTRATIONS BY
PAMELA QUERIN

BETHANY
BACKYARD®
www.bethanyhouse.com

Design and production: Lookout Design Group, Inc.

Printed in China.

Library of Congress Cataloging-in-Publication Data applied for

To Ariel Ashley,
our joy and delight—
a New Year's Day
granddaughter-gift from God.

—B . L .

To Mom, Dad, and Jeff
for always giving—
thank you for your love
and encouragement.

—P . Q .

*It is more blessed to give
than to receive.*

— A C T S   2 0 : 3 5

*I*t was the day before Christmas Eve.

Annika scraped hardened puddles of candle wax off the mantel.
Daydreams filled her head. Dreams of Christmas Eve dinner. Dreams
of rice pudding.

And . . . the almond.

Ten long years Annika had hoped for it, and now only one day
remained. One more day to wish and dream.

5

*E*rik, her brother, broke the stillness as he tap-danced a red yo-yo on the gleaming wood floor.

"Give it back, it's mine," little Davy called, reaching for the yo-yo with his crutch. As he did, he brushed against the gingerbread houses on the coffee table. Two fat gingerbread men toppled over.

"O-oh, careful." Annika scurried over to rescue her bread men. Frosty-white buttons sparkled on their gingerbread tummies.

Signs of Christmas shone through the house. A star glistened atop the tree, and evergreen boughs framed the mantel. Gilded apples and walnuts hung in clusters from pine boughs.

And there were candles, one in each window, to light the way for Jesus, the Christ child.

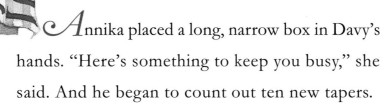

Annika placed a long, narrow box in Davy's hands. "Here's something to keep you busy," she said. And he began to count out ten new tapers.

Smells of freshly baked saffron buns drifted in from the kitchen. He sniffed the soothing aroma. "When will Mama cook the rice pudding for us?"

"Tomorrow morning," Annika said, lining up the candles along the mantel.

"I hope to find the almond in my pudding . . . this year," Davy said.

"No, no! I want the almond," shouted Erik.

Davy sat near the fire and sighed. "Cousin Ingrid got a new pair of snowshoes after *she* found the almond."

Annika straightened
a straw angel on the tree,
listening…dreaming. She went
to sit on the hearth, stroking
Davy's blond curls. "Papa says
it is God who grants our
wishes. But it's fun to dream,"
she whispered.

Davy leaned against her,
nodding. His angel-eyes shone
brightly.

December twenty-fourth dawned as sunlight ribbons wrapped the Christmas snow.

Annika scampered to the window, squinting out through the curtains. White mounds piled up on each roof like soft, white bread dough.

"What would I wish for?" she wondered aloud. "If ever I found the almond in my pudding . . . what would be my wish?"

Delectable, sweet notions teased her thoughts. A mountain of truffles coated with cocoa, perhaps? Enormous bowls of peppermint ice cream?

Sighing deeply, Annika considered her truest yearning. A secret wish to be sure.

Above all else, she longed for a dashing black pony. A pony to ride . . . with the wind.

Tappity-tap-tap. Downstairs came gentle knocking. Annika snatched up her bathrobe and flew to answer the front door.

A group of school friends stood on the snowy steps. Their voices rang out, *"God Jul!"* as they presented a plateful of star cookies.

"Merry Christmas to you," Annika said, accepting the sweets. "Come inside and warm up a bit."

Erik came into the parlor, rubbing his sleepy eyes. Davy appeared next, his crutch tucked under his arm. Annika and her friends gathered around the tree, admiring its handmade ornaments. "Tonight's the night for rice pudding," she announced with glee.

"Don't forget the almond," one girl remarked.

"It's never been in *my* pudding," Erik complained.

Annika nodded. "The almond has tricked me, too. My whole life."

"I got my wish," said one of the girls. "An adorable new kitten . . . the year I had the almond."

Davy leaned heavily on his crutch, attending to every word.

Soon Mama appeared, wearing a smock apron. "Merry Christmas to all of you," she greeted the girls, smiling. Then she motioned to Annika. "I'm ready for your help now, dear."

Annika and her friends said their goodbyes. Outside, the children called back their holiday wishes as sunbeams kissed their heads.

Hurrying to the kitchen, Annika helped stir the simmering white rice. She crossed her fingers behind her back as Mama mixed in the heavy cream. And, finally . . . a single almond.

Please, God, let it be my year, she prayed.

*T*hat evening, relatives chattered in the living room while tapers twinkled on the mantel.

"We welcome you to share our smorgasbord," Papa said, showing the guests to the kitchen, where the Christmas ham, red cabbage, tart applesauce, and sweet sausages were laid out on a sideboard.

The dining room table shone under a coppery glow. Davy, wearing an elf hat, was seated first.

Papa prayed a Christmas blessing, then speared a piece of rye bread with his fork. He dipped it into a kettle of hot pork and sausage drippings.

Davy wiggled impatiently. "Why do we do this every Christmas Eve?" he asked Annika.

"Because it's Swedish tradition," she whispered back.

There was hope in her brother's eyes, and he shivered momentarily.

The feast began with codfish, served with boiled potatoes and white sauce. Annika's feet danced under the table. It was hard to eat fish when her thoughts were on the almond.

$\mathcal{A}$t last, it was time for the children's rice pudding.

Davy trembled, holding his stomach. "Oh, Mama, I feel sick," he said.

Promptly, Papa came around the table and gathered the boy in his arms.

Mama reassured the guests. "The child is much too excited. That is all."

Annika peered down the long table as grown-ups chattered endlessly, passing desserts. She could scarcely wait another minute. So she set her silver spoon on top of the steaming white pudding.

Clink! A faint sound came from beneath a slight rise. She looked more closely. Annika caught her breath. There was an almond-shaped bump in her pudding!

Across the table, Erik swished his spoon through his bowl, searching. She opened her mouth to speak—to announce her grand discovery. But Papa's footsteps were in the hall, wrapped around Davy's timid voice.

Her heart thumped heavily. Beneath the pudding, inches from her hand, the almond lay hidden. She stared at the dish and the spoon concealing the tiny mound. Annika's secret wish pranced through her head.

Papa's footsteps grew louder, filling the hallway. Glancing up, she saw her brother clinging to Papa, eyes wide with expectation.

She struggled with fanciful thoughts, fairyland dreams. The beautiful ebony pony....

What would make Davy most happy this Christmas? she wondered.

Dear little brother. How he longed to run and play, to walk without a crutch. And finding the almond would surely make his heart glad.

In contrast, she thought of owning a dazzling pony. Of bounding through the meadow, the wind in her hair. *What would Jesus want me to do?* she wondered.

*S*he hesitated for only a moment. Then, without ever being noticed, Annika traded her dessert dish for her little brother's. The silver spoon remained atop the untouched pudding.

Soon, Papa brought the boy around to be seated. Reaching for his spoon, Davy scooped into the pudding. His laughter was strong and true. "The almond! I found the almond!"

Annika clapped her hands with the others and put on her best smile.

"Make a wish, darling boy," said Mama.

$\mathcal{A}$ll eyes were on Davy. Annika held her breath, as though holding it might make her brother's wish come true.

In one swift motion, Davy raised the spoon and the almond triumphantly over his fuzzy hat, toppling his wooden crutch to the floor. He pinched up his face and whispered, "I hope and pray for…" His gentle voice trailed away.

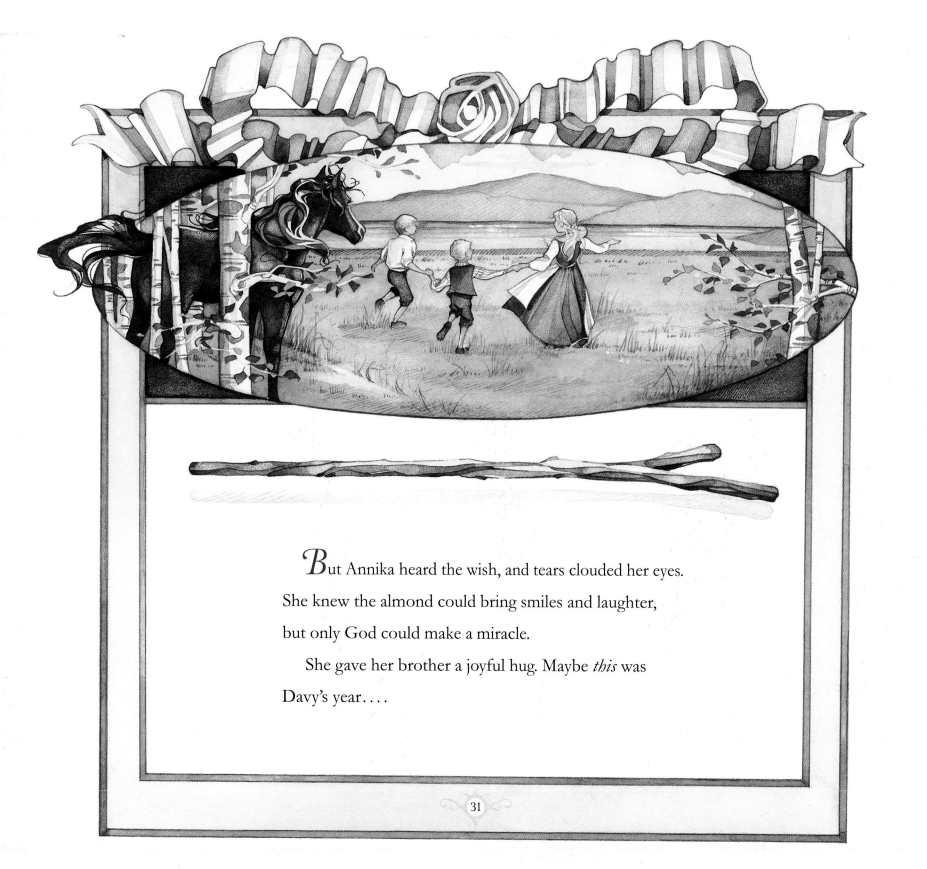

But Annika heard the wish, and tears clouded her eyes.
She knew the almond could bring smiles and laughter,
but only God could make a miracle.

She gave her brother a joyful hug. Maybe *this* was
Davy's year....

31

*L*ong ago in Sweden, Christmas Eve dinner began with sun-cured fish and ham, topped off with boiled rice pudding. Discovering the single almond in one's dessert dish was a much-anticipated moment for young and old alike.

A few days before Christmas, straw angels and star ornaments were handmade for the tree, representing the angelic announcement to the shepherds and the Star of Bethlehem. Children were encouraged to make Advent calendars, too, including pictures of the wise men's gifts to baby Jesus. The "Christmas crib," or manger, was placed in a prominent location, surrounded by hand-painted clay figures of Mary, Joseph, and three wise men.

On Christmas Day, Scandinavian Christians traveled by horse-drawn sleigh to celebrate Jesus' birthday at early-morning church services.